MAD  LIBS®

HANUKKAH MAD LIBS

concept created by Roger Price & Leonard Stern

Mad Libs
An Imprint of Penguin Random House

MAD LIBS
Penguin Young Readers Group
An Imprint of Penguin Random House LLC

Mad Libs format and text copyright © 2012 by Penguin Random House LLC. All rights reserved.

Concept created by Roger Price & Leonard Stern

Published by Mad Libs,
an imprint of Penguin Random House LLC,
345 Hudson Street, New York, New York 10014.
Printed in the USA.

ISBN 9780843172454
7 9 10 8 6

MAD LIBS
INSTRUCTIONS

MAD LIBS® is a game for people who don't like games!
It can be played by one, two, three, four, or forty.

• RIDICULOUSLY SIMPLE DIRECTIONS

In this tablet you will find stories containing blank spaces where words
are left out. One player, the READER, selects one of these stories. The
READER does not tell anyone what the story is about. Instead, he/she asks
the other players, the WRITERS, to give him/her words. These words are
used to fill in the blank spaces in the story.

• TO PLAY

The READER asks each WRITER in turn to call out a word—an adjective or
a noun or whatever the space calls for—and uses them to fill in the blank
spaces in the story. The result is a MAD LIBS® game.

When the READER then reads the completed MAD LIBS® game to the other
players, they will discover that they have written a story that is fantastic,
screamingly funny, shocking, silly, crazy, or just plain dumb—depending
upon which words each WRITER called out.

• EXAMPLE (*Before* and *After*)

"_____!" he said _____
     EXCLAMATION   ADVERB

as he jumped into his convertible _____ and
                                      NOUN

drove off with his _____ wife.
                    ADJECTIVE

"*Ouch*!" he said *Stupidly*
     EXCLAMATION   ADVERB

as he jumped into his convertible *cat* and
                                   NOUN

drove off with his *brave* wife.
                    ADJECTIVE

In case you have forgotten what adjectives, adverbs, nouns, and verbs are, here is a quick review:

An ADJECTIVE describes something or somebody. *Lumpy*, *soft*, *ugly*, *messy*, and *short* are adjectives.

An ADVERB tells how something is done. It modifies a verb and usually ends in "ly." *Modestly*, *stupidly*, *greedily*, and *carefully* are adverbs.

A NOUN is the name of a person, place, or thing. *Sidewalk*, *umbrella*, *bridle*, *bathtub*, and *nose* are nouns.

A VERB is an action word. *Run*, *pitch*, *jump*, and *swim* are verbs. Put the verbs in past tense if the directions say PAST TENSE. *Ran*, *pitched*, *jumped*, and *swam* are verbs in the past tense.

When we ask for A PLACE, we mean any sort of place: a country or city (*Spain*, *Cleveland*) or a room (*bathroom*, *kitchen*).

An EXCLAMATION or SILLY WORD is any sort of funny sound, gasp, grunt, or outcry, like *Wow!*, *Ouch!*, *Whomp!*, *Ick!*, and *Gadzooks!*

When we ask for specific words, like a NUMBER, a COLOR, an ANIMAL, or a PART OF THE BODY, we mean a word that is one of those things, like *seven*, *blue*, *horse*, or *head*.

When we ask for a PLURAL, it means more than one. For example, *cat* pluralized is *cats*.

MAD LIBS® is fun to play with friends, but you can also play it by yourself! To begin with, DO NOT look at the story on the page below. Fill in the blanks on this page with the words called for. Then, using the words you have selected, fill in the blank spaces in the story.

Now you've created your own hilarious MAD LIBS® game!

LATKE RECIPE

ADJECTIVE _____

ADJECTIVE _____

ADVERB _____

VERB _____

ADJECTIVE _____

NOUN _____

PLURAL NOUN _____

NOUN _____

TYPE OF LIQUID _____

ADJECTIVE _____

VERB _____

NOUN _____

COLOR _____

PLURAL NOUN _____

ADJECTIVE _____

MAD LIBS

LATKE RECIPE

What is the secret to making _____ latkes? Follow
                       ADJECTIVE

this _____ recipe to find out! Peel and _____
  ADJECTIVE   ADVERB

grate the potatoes. Transfer them into cold water, then allow

them to _____ until they are _____. In
        VERB   ADJECTIVE

a medium-sized _____, stir the potatoes, onions,
                 NOUN

_____, and _____ together. Pour some
   PLURAL NOUN   NOUN

_____ into a large skillet over high heat. Make sure it's
 TYPE OF LIQUID

good and _____ before you add the potatoes because
         ADJECTIVE

you don't want them to _____ while cooking. Press
                 VERB

down on them to form a/an _____ about 1/2 inch
                    NOUN

thick. Cook them until one side is _____ and then flip them
                           COLOR

over. Finally, let them drain on paper _____ and serve
                         PLURAL NOUN

_____!
  ADJECTIVE

MAD LIBS® is fun to play with friends, but you can also play it by yourself! To begin with, DO NOT look at the story on the page below. Fill in the blanks on this page with the words called for. Then, using the words you have selected, fill in the blank spaces in the story.

Now you've created your own hilarious MAD LIBS® game!

HOW TO PLAY DREIDEL

VERB _____

LETTER OF THE ALPHABET _____

NOUN _____

PLURAL NOUN _____

NOUN _____

ADVERB _____

PLURAL NOUN _____

PLURAL NOUN _____

PLURAL NOUN _____

PLURAL NOUN _____

ADJECTIVE _____

PLURAL NOUN _____

The Hebrew word for dreidel is *sevivon*, whose root word means "to

_____." Dreidels have four Hebrew letters on them—
    VERB

Nun, *Gimel*, *Hey*, and _____. They stand for the
                        LETTER OF THE ALPHABET

words "A great _____ happened there." Each player
                NOUN

starts out with the same number of game pieces, which can be

pennies, chocolate chips, or even _____. At the beginning
                                 PLURAL NOUN

of every round, each player antes up one _____,
                                          NOUN

then they take turns _____ spinning the dreidel. If
                     ADVERB

the dreidel lands on *Nun*, the player neither gives nor takes any

_____ from the pot. If a player spins a *Gimel*, he
    PLURAL NOUN

gets to take all the _____ for himself. If the dreidel
                     PLURAL NOUN

lands on *Hey*, the player takes half the _____, and
                                          PLURAL NOUN

if it lands on *Shin*, the player has to pay two _____
                                                  PLURAL NOUN

into the pot. Once a player runs out of game pieces, that player is

"_____." The game is over when one person has won
    ADJECTIVE

all the _____ for himself or herself!
        PLURAL NOUN

MAD LIBS® is fun to play with friends, but you can also play it by yourself! To begin with, DO NOT look at the story on the page below. Fill in the blanks on this page with the words called for. Then, using the words you have selected, fill in the blank spaces in the story.

Now you've created your own hilarious MAD LIBS® game!

SONG LYRICS:
"I HAVE A LITTLE DREIDEL"

NOUN _____

ADJECTIVE _____

VERB _____

PLURAL NOUN _____

NOUN _____

VERB _____

NOUN _____

ADJECTIVE _____

VERB _____

PLURAL NOUN _____

NOUN _____

VERB _____

MAD LIBS®
SONG LYRICS:
"I HAVE A LITTLE DREIDEL"

I have a little _____. I made it out of clay.
                    NOUN

And when it's dry and _____, oh dreidel I shall _____!
                        ADJECTIVE   VERB

Oh dreidel, dreidel, dreidel, I made it out of _____.
                                                PLURAL NOUN

Dreidel, dreidel, _____, oh dreidel I shall _____!
                    NOUN   VERB

It has a lovely _____ with legs so short and _____,
                  NOUN   ADJECTIVE

and when it gets all tired, it drops and then I _____!
                                                 VERB

Oh dreidel, dreidel, dreidel, I made it out of _____.
                                                PLURAL NOUN

Dreidel, dreidel, _____, oh dreidel I shall _____!
                    NOUN   VERB

MAD LIBS® is fun to play with friends, but you can also play it by yourself! To begin with, DO NOT look at the story on the page below. Fill in the blanks on this page with the words called for. Then, using the words you have selected, fill in the blank spaces in the story.

Now you've created your own hilarious MAD LIBS® game!

HANUKKAH AT MY HOUSE

NOUN _____

NOUN _____

ADJECTIVE _____

PLURAL NOUN _____

PART OF THE BODY (PLURAL) _____

ADJECTIVE _____

NUMBER _____

TYPE OF FOOD _____

PLURAL NOUN _____

PLURAL NOUN _____

VERB ENDING IN "ING" _____

NOUN _____

MAD LIBS

HANUKKAH AT MY HOUSE

In my family, each person gets to light one _____ on the

NOUN

menorah. Then we sing songs like "_____ of Ages."

NOUN

Afterward, Mom serves _____ treats like potato

ADJECTIVE

_____ and doughnuts, and we all eat until our

PLURAL NOUN

_____ are full. Along with _____ gifts,

PART OF THE BODY (PLURAL)   ADJECTIVE

it's traditional to give money on Hanukkah, so each night my father

gives all us kids _____ dollars! We play games like dreidel

NUMBER

and "Toss the _____." Then comes my favorite part: We

TYPE OF FOOD

open all the beautifully wrapped _____ that we bought

PLURAL NOUN

for one another. This year I gave my sister some _____ to

PLURAL NOUN

go with her dollhouse, and I got some _____

VERB ENDING IN "ING"

blocks for my brother. I can't wait to see what I got this year. I hope

it's a pet _____!

NOUN

MAD LIBS® is fun to play with friends, but you can also play it by yourself! To begin with, DO NOT look at the story on the page below. Fill in the blanks on this page with the words called for. Then, using the words you have selected, fill in the blank spaces in the story.

Now you've created your own hilarious MAD LIBS® game!

HANUKKAH QUIZ

NUMBER _____

NOUN _____

CELEBRITY _____

NUMBER _____

TYPE OF LIQUID _____

PLURAL NOUN _____

PLURAL NOUN _____

A PLACE _____

SILLY WORD _____

NOUN _____

NOUN _____

MAD LIBS®

HANUKKAH QUIZ

How much do you really know about Hanukkah? Take this true or

false quiz and find out if you're a hero or a/an _____!
                                                    NUMBER

1. The name *Maccabee* means _____. True or false?
                               NOUN

2. The villain of Hanukkah was _____. True or false?
                                CELEBRITY

3. We celebrate Hanukkah for _____ days because
                              NUMBER

   that's how long the _____ lasted. True or false?
                        TYPE OF LIQUID

4. Hanukkah celebrates the victory of the _____ over
                                           PLURAL NOUN

   the _____. True or false?
        PLURAL NOUN

5. The Maccabees were from (the) _____. True or false?
                                  A PLACE

6. The Hebrew word for *dreidel* is _____. True or false?
                                     SILLY WORD

You can find the answers in the back of the _____. If you
                                             NOUN

scored 100 percent, congratulations! You're a Hanukkah _____!
                                                        NOUN

MAD LIBS® is fun to play with friends, but you can also play it by yourself! To begin with, DO NOT look at the story on the page below. Fill in the blanks on this page with the words called for. Then, using the words you have selected, fill in the blank spaces in the story.

Now you've created your own hilarious MAD LIBS® game!

HANUKKAH SCAVENGER HUNT

ADJECTIVE _____

PERSON IN ROOM (FEMALE) _____

PLURAL NOUN _____

PLURAL NOUN _____

ADVERB _____

NOUN _____

VERB _____

ADVERB _____

A PLACE _____

ADJECTIVE _____

TYPE OF FOOD _____

EXCLAMATION _____

NOUN _____

ADJECTIVE _____

VERB ENDING IN "ING" _____

MAD LIBS®
HANUKKAH
SCAVENGER HUNT

This year my parents created a really _____ scavenger
                                          ADJECTIVE

hunt for me and my sister _____. We had to follow
                          PERSON IN ROOM (FEMALE)

clues in order to find our _____ at the end. The first
                              PLURAL NOUN

clue said, "Hanukkah is known as the Festival of what?" I knew the

answer was _____, so I _____ went to the
              PLURAL NOUN   ADVERB

menorah. Inside the box of candles, I found a/an _____
                                                      NOUN

that said, "Find the toy that likes to _____." The answer
                                          VERB

was obviously a dreidel, so I _____ went over to (the)
                                  ADVERB

_____. Once there, I found the final clue. "Your present
   A PLACE

is hidden among some _____ treats." Immediately I saw
                        ADJECTIVE

a platter of _____ and thought, "_____!"
              TYPE OF FOOD   EXCLAMATION

Sure enough, I found a brand-new _____ inside, just
                                    NOUN

for me. This was the best Hanukkah ever because not only did

I get a/an _____ present, but I also got to have fun
              ADJECTIVE

_____ for it!
VERB ENDING IN "ING"

MAD LIBS® is fun to play with friends, but you can also play it by yourself! To begin with, DO NOT look at the story on the page below. Fill in the blanks on this page with the words called for. Then, using the words you have selected, fill in the blank spaces in the story.

Now you've created your own hilarious MAD LIBS® game!

HANUKKAH PARTY AT BUBBE'S

PLURAL NOUN _____

ADJECTIVE _____

NOUN _____

NOUN _____

ADJECTIVE _____

ADJECTIVE _____

PLURAL NOUN _____

PLURAL NOUN _____

ADJECTIVE _____

NOUN _____

ADJECTIVE _____

ADJECTIVE _____

PLURAL NOUN _____

VERB _____

EXCLAMATION _____

MAD LIBS®
HANUKKAH PARTY
AT BUBBE'S

I love going to my bubbe's house for Hanukkah because she makes

the best potato _____ in the whole, _____ world.
<u>PLURAL NOUN</u>   <u>ADJECTIVE</u>

"The secret," she says, "is to use freshly pressed _____
                                                        <u>NOUN</u>

oil." She serves them up on a/an _____, along with loads
                                      <u>NOUN</u>

of other _____ dishes and then orders everyone to "Get
            <u>ADJECTIVE</u>

'em while they're _____!" I love how Bubbe decorates
                       <u>ADJECTIVE</u>

the living room with blue-and-white _____ and always
                                          <u>PLURAL NOUN</u>

keeps an extra stash of chocolate _____ in the pantry
                                         <u>PLURAL NOUN</u>

for me and my _____ brother. She sits next to me on
                   <u>ADJECTIVE</u>

the _____ and sings _____ songs, buys me
        <u>NOUN</u>   <u>ADJECTIVE</u>

really _____ presents, and lets me watch all my favorite
           <u>ADJECTIVE</u>

_____ on TV. She also lets me _____
<u>PLURAL NOUN</u>   <u>VERB</u>

whenever I want to. Mom and Dad have to say no but Bubbe always

says, "_____!"
           <u>EXCLAMATION</u>

MAD LIBS® is fun to play with friends, but you can also play it by yourself! To begin with, DO NOT look at the story on the page below. Fill in the blanks on this page with the words called for. Then, using the words you have selected, fill in the blank spaces in the story.

Now you've created your own hilarious MAD LIBS® game!

WHY HANUKKAH IS MY FAVORITE HOLIDAY

PLURAL NOUN _____

PLURAL NOUN _____

NOUN _____

NOUN _____

NOUN _____

NUMBER _____

PLURAL NOUN _____

PLURAL NOUN _____

VERB _____

NOUN _____

NOUN _____

PLURAL NOUN _____

MAD LIBS®
WHY HANUKKAH IS
MY FAVORITE HOLIDAY

Hanukkah is my favorite holiday of the year because I get lots of

_____. No, wait! On Shavuot we get to make ice-
    PLURAL NOUN

cream _____ and eat _____ cake, so
            PLURAL NOUN   NOUN

Shavuot is definitely my favorite holiday. But wait! On Sukkot I get

to go in the backyard and build a/an _____ with my
                                            NOUN

dad, so I like Sukkot the best. Then again, on Passover I get to be the

_____ of the show and ask the _____ Questions.
    NOUN   NUMBER

And on Rosh Hashanah I get to dip _____ in honey,
                                        PLURAL NOUN

which I really like, so maybe . . . no—Tu B'Shevat is my favorite

holiday, I'm sure of it, because I get to plant _____ in the
                                                  PLURAL NOUN

ground. But then again, on Simchat Torah we all _____
                                                        VERB

with one another. On Shabbat my entire family gets together to

share a/an _____. On Purim I get to dress up as a/an
                NOUN

_____! I guess I can't pick a favorite. All the Jewish
        NOUN

holidays are more fun than a barrel of _____!
                                            PLURAL NOUN

MAD LIBS® is fun to play with friends, but you can also play it by yourself! To begin with, DO NOT look at the story on the page below. Fill in the blanks on this page with the words called for. Then, using the words you have selected, fill in the blank spaces in the story.

Now you've created your own hilarious MAD LIBS® game!

CELEBRATING
THE JEWISH HOLIDAYS 101

NOUN _____

ADJECTIVE _____

PLURAL NOUN _____

ADJECTIVE _____

NOUN _____

A PLACE _____

PERSON IN ROOM _____

ADJECTIVE _____

NOUN _____

NOUN _____

NOUN _____

VERB _____

NUMBER _____

ADJECTIVE _____

VERB _____

PLURAL NOUN _____

NOUN _____

MAD☺LIBS®
CELEBRATING
THE JEWISH HOLIDAYS 101

We all know how to celebrate Hanukkah—we light the _____,
NOUN

sing _____ songs, eat oily _____, and play dreidel.
ADJECTIVE PLURAL NOUN

But how do we celebrate some of the other _____
ADJECTIVE

holidays throughout the year? Well, on Tu B'Shevat, we celebrate by

planting a/an _____ in the ground or by donating money
NOUN

to an organization that plants trees in (the) _____.
A PLACE

To celebrate Purim, we read the Book of _____ and wear
PERSON IN ROOM

_____ costumes. On Passover we have a special meal
ADJECTIVE

called a Seder, which means "_____." Someone hides the
NOUN

_____ and all the kids try to find it at the end of the
NOUN

Seder. On Sukkot we build a/an _____ outside and then
NOUN

_____ in it for _____ days. There are many more
VERB NUMBER

holidays, but one of the most _____ is Shavuot. That's when
ADJECTIVE

we stay up and _____ all night long, and then the next day,
VERB

we listen to the reading of the Ten _____. I guess that's
PLURAL NOUN

why they call us the People of the _____!
NOUN

MAD LIBS® is fun to play with friends, but you can also play it by yourself! To begin with, DO NOT look at the story on the page below. Fill in the blanks on this page with the words called for. Then, using the words you have selected, fill in the blank spaces in the story.

Now you've created your own hilarious MAD LIBS® game!

HANUKKAH WISHES

ADJECTIVE _____

PLURAL NOUN _____

ADJECTIVE _____

PLURAL NOUN _____

PLURAL NOUN _____

PLURAL NOUN _____

NOUN _____

NOUN _____

VERB _____

PLURAL NOUN _____

ADJECTIVE _____

PLURAL NOUN _____

PLURAL NOUN _____

MAD LIBS

HANUKKAH WISHES

It has been an especially _____ Hanukkah for me
                        ADJECTIVE

this year. I am surrounded by friends, family, great food, and lots of

_____. I feel so thankful, and I consider myself especially
PLURAL NOUN

_____, so I'd like to share my Hanukkah wishes for
ADJECTIVE

you all: May your garden overflow with _____. May
                                        PLURAL NOUN

you receive many _____ from your children. May your
                  PLURAL NOUN

_____ be few and far between. May you always
PLURAL NOUN

have a/an _____ when you really need one. May your
          NOUN

_____ never show when you _____, and
NOUN   VERB

may you live out your days in health, wisdom, and with many

_____. I hope you have a/an _____ Hanukkah
PLURAL NOUN   ADJECTIVE

filled with the light and love of good _____ and
                                       PLURAL NOUN

finally . . . I hope you don't get indigestion from eating too many

_____!
PLURAL NOUN

MAD LIBS® is fun to play with friends, but you can also play it by yourself! To begin with, DO NOT look at the story on the page below. Fill in the blanks on this page with the words called for. Then, using the words you have selected, fill in the blank spaces in the story.

Now you've created your own hilarious MAD LIBS® game!

HANUKKAH CATALOG

ADJECTIVE _____

NOUN _____

NOUN _____

ADJECTIVE _____

PLURAL NOUN _____

PART OF THE BODY _____

NOUN _____

PLURAL NOUN _____

NOUN _____

CELEBRITY _____

ADJECTIVE _____

ADJECTIVE _____

PLURAL NOUN _____

PART OF THE BODY _____

PLURAL NOUN _____

A PLACE _____

While shopping for your _____ ones this holiday

ADJECTIVE

season, we here at the Hanukkah _____ know

NOUN

you want only the best. Please allow me to present, for your

consideration, this ceramic serving _____. It is so

NOUN

beautiful that you'll almost feel _____ when you pile

ADJECTIVE

it high with potato _____. Here is another unique and

PLURAL NOUN

_____-catching item: a/an _____-themed

PART OF THE BODY   NOUN

menorah that is sure to be a hit with your little _____.

PLURAL NOUN

What do you get for the bubbe who has everything? A mah-jongg-

themed _____, of course! And how about Zeyde?

NOUN

This biography of _____ will keep him _____ for

CELEBRITY   ADJECTIVE

hours! When shopping for that _____ someone in your life,

ADJECTIVE

don't forget to check out our complete line of _____.

PLURAL NOUN

They are all _____-painted by _____ in

PART OF THE BODY   PLURAL NOUN

(the) _____!

A PLACE

MAD LIBS® is fun to play with friends, but you can also play it by yourself! To begin with, DO NOT look at the story on the page below. Fill in the blanks on this page with the words called for. Then, using the words you have selected, fill in the blank spaces in the story.

Now you've created your own hilarious MAD LIBS® game!

HOW TO LIGHT THE MENORAH

ADJECTIVE _____

PLURAL NOUN _____

PLURAL NOUN _____

ADJECTIVE _____

NOUN _____

PLURAL NOUN _____

NOUN _____

NOUN _____

NOUN _____

VERB ENDING IN "ING" _____

ADJECTIVE _____

PLURAL NOUN _____

MAD LIBS®
HOW TO LIGHT
THE MENORAH

Lighting the menorah is the most _____ part of celebrating

ADJECTIVE

Hanukkah. The whole family gathers around and is reminded of

the miracle of the eight _____. In order to perform the

PLURAL NOUN

lighting ceremony, you will need a menorah, _____

PLURAL NOUN

that fit in your menorah, and matches to light them. The candles

of the menorah can be in a/an _____ line. The menorah

ADJECTIVE

should be placed on a/an _____ so that it can be seen by as

NOUN

many _____ as possible. On the first night of Hanukkah,

PLURAL NOUN

place a candle in the _____ on your menorah. This is

NOUN

called the *shamash*, or _____, and you always light it first.

NOUN

Then place a/an _____ in the rightmost position on your

NOUN

menorah, and use the *shamash* to light it. After _____,

VERB ENDING IN "ING"

you can sing songs, eat _____ foods, and open

ADJECTIVE

_____!

PLURAL NOUN

MAD LIBS® is fun to play with friends, but you can also play it by yourself! To begin with, DO NOT look at the story on the page below. Fill in the blanks on this page with the words called for. Then, using the words you have selected, fill in the blank spaces in the story.

Now you've created your own hilarious MAD LIBS® game!

EIGHT NIGHTS OF GIFTS

ARTICLE OF CLOTHING (PLURAL) _____

LAST NAME _____

NOUN _____

PLURAL NOUN _____

PERSON IN ROOM _____

TYPE OF FOOD _____

ADJECTIVE _____

NUMBER _____

ARTICLE OF CLOTHING (PLURAL) _____

NOUN _____

LETTER OF THE ALPHABET _____

VERB _____

PLURAL NOUN _____

EIGHT NIGHTS OF GIFTS

On the first night of Hanukkah, I got a T-shirt and a pair of

_____ from my parents. Lame! The second
ARTICLE OF CLOTHING (PLURAL)

night I got a DVD—*Harry* _____ *and*
LAST NAME

the Sorcerer's _____ ! On nights three and four I got
NOUN

_____ to use at school, which is great because I had been
PLURAL NOUN

borrowing from my friend _____. The fifth night I got
PERSON IN ROOM

a/an _____ tower from my bubbe. She's always giving us
TYPE OF FOOD

_____ treats. On the sixth night my father gave me some
ADJECTIVE

gelt —_____ dollars to be exact. The seventh night I got
NUMBER

two new _____. And then for the big finale . . .
ARTICLE OF CLOTHING (PLURAL)

on the eighth night I got a wireless _____ to go with
NOUN

my _____-Box Live! I was so excited I could hardly
LETTER OF THE ALPHABET

_____ ! I know that Hanukkah isn't really about how
VERB

many _____ you get, but boy do they make it fun!
PLURAL NOUN

MAD LIBS® is fun to play with friends, but you can also play it by yourself! To begin with, DO NOT look at the story on the page below. Fill in the blanks on this page with the words called for. Then, using the words you have selected, fill in the blank spaces in the story.

Now you've created your own hilarious MAD LIBS® game!

THE MALL

PART OF THE BODY _____

NUMBER _____

NOUN _____

PART OF THE BODY _____

NOUN _____

NOUN _____

VERB (PAST TENSE) _____

ADJECTIVE _____

NOUN _____

PART OF THE BODY (PLURAL) _____

NOUN _____

NOUN _____

NUMBER _____

EXCLAMATION _____

MAD LIBS

THE MALL

I couldn't decide what to get my girlfriend for Hanukkah this year, so

I decided to browse our local mall and hope something would catch

my _____. But it took at least _____
    PART OF THE BODY   NUMBER

minutes to find a parking spot for my _____ because
                                         NOUN

the lot was so crowded. Once inside, I found myself shoulder-

to-_____ with all the other shoppers, and let me tell
  PART OF THE BODY

you, it was dog-cat-_____ and every _____
                    NOUN   NOUN

for himself! I pushed and _____ my way into a few
                           VERB (PAST TENSE)

shops, but couldn't find anything _____. After a few
                                ADJECTIVE

hours, I wondered if I should just throw in the _____.
                                     NOUN

But then, there it was, right before my very _____:
                              PART OF THE BODY (PLURAL)

a brand-new, shiny, top-of-the-_____, state-of-the-art
                              NOUN

_____! I felt a mixture of excitement and relief . . . until
  NOUN

I saw the price. _____ dollars?? _____!
                NUMBER   EXCLAMATION

Next year I'm shopping online.

MAD LIBS® is fun to play with friends, but you can also play it by yourself! To begin with, DO NOT look at the story on the page below. Fill in the blanks on this page with the words called for. Then, using the words you have selected, fill in the blank spaces in the story.

Now you've created your own hilarious MAD LIBS® game!

TUMMY ACHE!

EXCLAMATION _____

PART OF THE BODY _____

VERB _____

TYPE OF FOOD _____

NUMBER _____

PLURAL NOUN _____

PLURAL NOUN _____

ADJECTIVE _____

PLURAL NOUN _____

NUMBER _____

A PLACE _____

ADJECTIVE _____

NOUN _____

PART OF THE BODY _____

ADJECTIVE _____

NOUN _____

ADJECTIVE _____

MAD LIBS®

TUMMY ACHE!

_____! I have the worst _____-ache
   EXCLAMATION   PART OF THE BODY

and can hardly _____. I don't understand why—all
              VERB

I ate tonight was one potato _____. Okay, maybe it
              TYPE OF FOOD

was more like _____, but still, that's not very many. I did
      NUMBER

taste the jelly _____, and I guess I tried the sugar-coated
      PLURAL NOUN

_____, too, but they looked so _____ I
   PLURAL NOUN   ADJECTIVE

couldn't resist. Oh, and then there were the fried _____
              PLURAL NOUN

that my aunt made—I had _____ of those. But she came
         NUMBER

to visit all the way from (the) _____, and it would have
         A PLACE

been _____ manners not to have at least one. My mom
  ADJECTIVE

brought out some _____ sorbet after the meal, which
       NOUN

she said would "cleanse the _____," and then she served
        PART OF THE BODY

_____ coffee. I didn't have the coffee, but I did have a
 ADJECTIVE

few glasses of _____ juice. So you see, it doesn't make any
      NOUN

sense for me to feel _____ right now. I barely ate anything!
      ADJECTIVE

MAD LIBS® is fun to play with friends, but you can also play it by yourself! To begin with, DO NOT look at the story on the page below. Fill in the blanks on this page with the words called for. Then, using the words you have selected, fill in the blank spaces in the story.

Now you've created your own hilarious MAD LIBS® game!

GRANDPARENTS KNOW EVERYTHING

PERSON IN ROOM _____

PERSON IN ROOM _____

SILLY WORD _____

NOUN _____

PLURAL NOUN _____

NOUN _____

ADJECTIVE _____

LETTER OF THE ALPHABET _____

NOUN _____

A PLACE _____

NOUN _____

NOUN _____

MAD LIBS
GRANDPARENTS
KNOW EVERYTHING

The following is a dialogue to be performed by _____
<u>PERSON IN ROOM</u>

and _____:
<u>PERSON IN ROOM</u>

Child: "Why do we call Hanukkah the Festival of Lights?"

Grandfather: "Well, my little _____, it would be
<u>SILLY WORD</u>

pretty silly to call it the Commemoration of the _____
<u>NOUN</u>

or the Miracle of the Eight _____, wouldn't it?"
<u>PLURAL NOUN</u>

Child: "Yeah, I guess so. And how come we eat potato pancakes?"

Grandfather: "Because they're tastier than _____ pancakes."
<u>NOUN</u>

Child: "Oh. What are these _____-looking symbols
<u>ADJECTIVE</u>

on my dreidel?"

Grandfather: "They are the Hebrew letters *Nun, Gimel, Hey,* and

_____. They stand for 'A great _____
<u>LETTER OF THE ALPHABET</u>   <u>NOUN</u>

happened in (the) _____.'"
<u>A PLACE</u>

Child: "Thanks! You sure do know a lot about Hanukkah."

Grandfather: "Smart as a/an _____ and sharp as a/an
<u>NOUN</u>

_____—your old gramps has still got it!"
<u>NOUN</u>

MAD LIBS® is fun to play with friends, but you can also play it by yourself! To begin with, DO NOT look at the story on the page below. Fill in the blanks on this page with the words called for. Then, using the words you have selected, fill in the blank spaces in the story.

Now you've created your own hilarious MAD LIBS® game!

BEST HANUKKAH BOOKS

NOUN _____

PLURAL NOUN _____

PERSON IN ROOM _____

PLURAL NOUN _____

VERB _____

PLURAL NOUN _____

NOUN _____

VERB ENDING IN "ING" _____

PERSON IN ROOM _____

ADJECTIVE _____

PLURAL NOUN _____

NOUN _____

PART OF THE BODY _____

ADJECTIVE _____

NOUN _____

ADJECTIVE _____

NOUN _____

MAD LIBS®

BEST HANUKKAH BOOKS

Hanukkah is right around the _____, so stock up on
                                        NOUN

this year's best literary _____. In comedy, we have
                                   PLURAL NOUN

_____ *and the Hanukkah* _____. I guarantee
PERSON IN ROOM   PLURAL NOUN

you'll _____ yourself silly. In mystery, we have *Who Stole*
              VERB

the Hanukkah _____? You'll be trying to guess who did
                      PLURAL NOUN

it right up until the final _____ is revealed! The latest
                                      NOUN

romance from best-_____ author _____ is
                        VERB ENDING IN "ING"   PERSON IN ROOM

called *The* _____ *Dreidel of Love and* _____.
                  ADJECTIVE   PLURAL NOUN

I warn you, though, it's a/an _____-jerker that will
                                        NOUN

tug at your _____-strings. For girls, we have *The*
                PART OF THE BODY

Princess and the _____ *Menorah*, while boys might
                          ADJECTIVE

enjoy *A Pirate's Hanukkah* _____. And if you just want
                                    NOUN

something completely _____, check out the world's
                              ADJECTIVE

first Hanukkah-themed science fiction novel, *The Great Galactic*

Hanukkah _____!
                NOUN

MAD LIBS® is fun to play with friends, but you can also play it by yourself! To begin with, DO NOT look at the story on the page below. Fill in the blanks on this page with the words called for. Then, using the words you have selected, fill in the blank spaces in the story.

Now you've created your own hilarious MAD LIBS® game!

HANUKKAH CRAFT IDEAS

ADJECTIVE _____

PLURAL NOUN _____

NOUN _____

ADVERB _____

PLURAL NOUN _____

ADJECTIVE _____

NOUN _____

NOUN _____

ADJECTIVE _____

PLURAL NOUN _____

NOUN _____

VERB ENDING IN "ING" _____

NOUN _____

NOUN _____

PART OF THE BODY (PLURAL) _____

PLURAL NOUN _____

PLURAL NOUN _____

ADJECTIVE _____

PLURAL NOUN _____

MAD LIBS®

HANUKKAH CRAFT IDEAS

Hanukkah is a/an _____ time to do arts and
                            ADJECTIVE

_____ with your kids. You can make your own
       PLURAL NOUN

menorah by covering a wooden _____ with tinfoil and
                                      NOUN

then _____ taping it closed. Then let your child
           ADVERB

glue eight _____ to it, and light them up! Another
              PLURAL NOUN

_____ craft idea is to print out a/an _____
  ADJECTIVE   NOUN

template and have your child color it in. This will be easy for

your little _____ to do, and it always turns out super-
               NOUN

_____. If you have older _____, there are many
  ADJECTIVE   PLURAL NOUN

more sophisticated crafts you can do with them. You can make a/an

_____ out of _____ clay or an origami
     NOUN   VERB ENDING IN "ING"

_____ of David. Or make a/an _____ out of
     NOUN   NOUN

foam, and then glue googly _____ on it for a fun
                            PART OF THE BODY (PLURAL)

Hanukkah decoration. Try decorating Hanukkah cookies with

_____ or making a dreidel out of _____.
  PLURAL NOUN   PLURAL NOUN

With a/an _____ imagination, the _____
             ADJECTIVE   PLURAL NOUN

are endless!

MAD LIBS® is fun to play with friends, but you can also play it by yourself! To begin with, DO NOT look at the story on the page below. Fill in the blanks on this page with the words called for. Then, using the words you have selected, fill in the blank spaces in the story.

Now you've created your own hilarious MAD LIBS® game!

HANUKKAH GAMES

PLURAL NOUN _____

PLURAL NOUN _____

NOUN _____

PLURAL NOUN _____

PLURAL NOUN _____

ADJECTIVE _____

ADJECTIVE _____

PLURAL NOUN _____

ADJECTIVE _____

PLURAL NOUN _____

NOUN _____

ADJECTIVE _____

PLURAL NOUN _____

ADJECTIVE _____

VERB ENDING IN "ING" _____

MAD LIBS®
HANUKKAH GAMES

Ever get tired of the same old Hanukkah games? Spice them up by

adding new twists and _____! When playing dreidel, use

_____ PLURAL NOUN

_____ instead of pennies. You can put a Hanukkah twist

PLURAL NOUN

on a classic game and play Pin the Candle on the _____.

NOUN

Put on some klezmer music and play musical _____.

PLURAL NOUN

If you have a computer, go to Hanukkah-_____.com

PLURAL NOUN

and play their selection of _____ games. For a more

ADJECTIVE

_____ approach, create a card with pictures of Hanukkah

ADJECTIVE

_____ all over it and play bingo. A popular game is

PLURAL NOUN

anagrams: a very _____ pastime among _____.

ADJECTIVE PLURAL NOUN

Give everyone a pen and _____, and then give them a

NOUN

word related to the holiday, such as "_____." Then

ADJECTIVE

everyone has to find as many _____ as possible using

PLURAL NOUN

only the letters from that word. These games will have you and your

_____ ones laughing and _____ the whole

ADJECTIVE VERB ENDING IN "ING"

night through! *Chag Sameach!*

MAD LIBS® is fun to play with friends, but you can also play it by yourself! To begin with, DO NOT look at the story on the page below. Fill in the blanks on this page with the words called for. Then, using the words you have selected, fill in the blank spaces in the story.

Now you've created your own hilarious MAD LIBS® game!

HOW TO HOST THE PERFECT HANUKKAH PARTY

CELEBRITY _____

NOUN _____

PLURAL NOUN _____

VERB _____

PLURAL NOUN _____

VERB _____

ADJECTIVE _____

NOUN _____

VERB _____

PLURAL NOUN _____

ADVERB _____

NOUN _____

NOUN _____

PLURAL NOUN _____

ADJECTIVE _____

ADJECTIVE _____

ADJECTIVE _____

NOUN _____

MAD LIBS®
HOW TO HOST THE PERFECT HANUKKAH PARTY

You don't have to be _____ to host the perfect Hanukkah
                          CELEBRITY

party. This year, host your own Hanukkah-themed _____!
                                                NOUN

First, enlist a friend to help you set up the _____ and
                                             PLURAL NOUN

_____ with you on the big night. Designate people to
VERB

bring drinks, salads, and _____. Then plan your menu.
                          PLURAL NOUN

If you're short on time, don't _____. There is no need
                              VERB

to drive yourself _____. You can always buy a frozen
                  ADJECTIVE

_____, let it _____, and then fry it up for your
NOUN   VERB

guests. Or you can buy ready-made _____ and bake them.
                                  PLURAL NOUN

You should _____ go all out with the decorations, though,
           ADVERB

including a/an _____ on your door that says "Welcome
              NOUN

to the _____!" and some funky _____ on the
       NOUN   PLURAL NOUN

table. The decorations go a long way in creating a/an _____
                                                     ADJECTIVE

atmosphere for your guests. Put on some _____ music,
                                        ADJECTIVE

take a quick shower, get dressed in your most _____ outfit,
                                              ADJECTIVE

and get ready for a/an _____ to remember!
                       NOUN

MAD LIBS® is fun to play with friends, but you can also play it by yourself! To begin with, DO NOT look at the story on the page below. Fill in the blanks on this page with the words called for. Then, using the words you have selected, fill in the blank spaces in the story.

Now you've created your own hilarious MAD LIBS® game!

HANUKKAH IN HOLLYWOOD

LETTER OF THE ALPHABET _____

PLURAL NOUN _____

CELEBRITY _____

PLURAL NOUN _____

ADJECTIVE _____

CELEBRITY (MALE) _____

NOUN _____

A PLACE _____

EXCLAMATION _____

NOUN _____

CELEBRITY _____

A PLACE _____

PLURAL NOUN _____

CELEBRITY (FEMALE) _____

NOUN _____

NUMBER _____

PLURAL NOUN _____

MAD☺LIBS®
HANUKKAH
IN HOLLYWOOD

There are lots of _____-listers in Hollywood who
<small>LETTER OF THE ALPHABET</small>

celebrate the Festival of _____. For example, did
<small>PLURAL NOUN</small>

you know _____ lights a menorah made entirely of
<small>CELEBRITY</small>

_____? You might think that's _____,
<small>PLURAL NOUN</small> <small>ADJECTIVE</small>

but it's nothing compared to _____, who drives
<small>CELEBRITY (MALE)</small>

his _____ around (the) _____ each year,
<small>NOUN</small> <small>A PLACE</small>

shouting, "_____! It's Hanukkah!" Then there are more
<small>EXCLAMATION</small>

_____-driven stars, like _____, who make
<small>NOUN</small> <small>CELEBRITY</small>

appearances all over (the) _____ on Hanukkah to raise
<small>A PLACE</small>

money for nonprofits such as Save the _____. And you
<small>PLURAL NOUN</small>

will probably be surprised to learn that _____ actually
<small>CELEBRITY (FEMALE)</small>

makes her own latkes and _____ ball soup! If you made
<small>NOUN</small>

_____ dollars per film, how would you celebrate the
<small>NUMBER</small>

Festival of _____?
<small>PLURAL NOUN</small>